Sleepy Bleek

Om KIDZ
An imprint of Om Books International

Om KIDZ | Om Books International

Reprinted in 2025

Corporate & Editorial Office
A-12, Sector 64, Noida 201 301
Uttar Pradesh, India
Phone: +91 120 477 4100
Email: editorial@ombooks.com
Website: www.ombooksinternational.com

Sales Office
107, Ansari Road, Darya Ganj
New Delhi 110 002, India
Phone: +91 11 4000 9000
Email: sales@ombooks.com
Website: www.ombooks.com

ISBN: 978-93-85273-83-4

Printed in India

10 9 8 7 6 5

Sleepy Bleek

I'm all set to read

Paste your photograph here

My name is

____

Bleek is a very lazy **sheep**.
She lives on a peaceful, **green** farm.
All she wants to do is eat grass
and **sleep** all day.

Bleek the **sheep** is always looking for places to **sleep**. But no one lets her **sleep**. Poor **Bleek**! This makes her **feel** very tired.

Z Z Z
Z Z Z Z Z

After grazing in the **green** meadow,
Bleek is full and very **sleepy.**
She is **keen** on taking a nap.
So, she shuts her eyes for a **wee** while.

“Bzzzzzzzzzzzz!” Oh, no!
A **bee keeps** buzzing around **Bleek**.
Bleek doesn’t take **heed** of the **bee**.
The bee sits on **Bleek’s** nose.

Bleek can't sleep with a **bee** on her nose, so she goes back to the farm. The farm is **breezy** and **Bleek** falls into a **deep sleep**.

BEEP
BEEP

"Beep! Beep! Beep! Beep!"
The farmer **steers** his **jeep** into the farm, honking away. "**Eeeek!**" yells **Bleek** as she wakes up from her **sleep**.

Bleek cannot **sleep** on the farm, so she starts walking. Soon, she finds a **tree** and dozes under it. It gives her shade so **Bleek feels carefree**.

"Tap! Tap! Tap! Tap!" Standing near the **tree** is a shepherd, who keeps tapping his **feet**. **Bleek's sleep** is disturbed again because of all the tapping!

So **Bleek** walks around until she finds a barn and goes to **sleep** there. She can smell the **sweet** hay. It makes her **feel** peaceful.

"Swish! Swish! Swish!"
The farm boy is **sweeping** hay off the floor. This wakes **Bleek** again. Is there no place for **Bleek** to **sleep** peacefully?

Bleek needs to **sleep** as she is very tired. She is so drowsy that she is about to **weep**. She walks on **feebly**.

Bleek cannot find a place to **sleep**. So she climbs on to the **steep** roof of the farmer's house. The cool wind puts **Bleek** to **sleep** right away.

There are no **bees** or **jeeps**
on the roof to disturb **Bleek**.
No tapping **feet** or **sweeping**
farm boys will wake her up here.

Finally **Bleek** can rest her **cheek** upon her paw and **sleep**. The shepherd **tweets** his whistle to round up the **sheep**. But **Bleek** is fast **asleep**. **Sweet** dreams, **Bleek**!

Z Z

Know your phonic words

These words have the long "e" sound in them.

Bleek
sheep
keeps
green
deep
sleep
feel
keen
wee
heed
bee

breezy
beep
steers
jeep
Eeeek
tree
needs
carefree
sweet
sweeping
weep

feebly
steep
feet
cheek
tweets
asleep